►Special Days◄

Bonfire Night

Clare Chandler

WAYLAND

► Special Days ◄

Bonfire Night
May Day
Mother's Day
Poppy Day

Editor: Carron Brown
Designer: Kate Buxton
Illustrator: David Antram
Cover artwork: Barbara Loftus
Consultant: Norah Granger

First published in 1997 by Wayland Publishers Limited,
61 Western Road, Hove, East Sussex, BN3 1JD

Copyright © 1997 Wayland Publishers Limited

Find W_____ b_____ i_____ _____ h_____ _____ .co.uk

B_____

3. Great B_____ literature

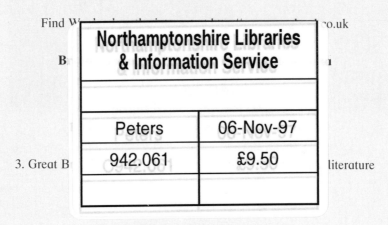

ISBN 0 7502 2041 4

Typeset by Kate Buxton
Printed and bound by G. Canale and C.S.p.A in Turin, Italy

Picture Acknowledgements
The publishers would like to thank the following for allowing us to reproduce their pictures: British Museum *cover*, 6, 30;
Mary Evans Picture Library 28, 29; Hulton Getty 11; Icorec (Circa Photo Library/John Smith) 8; National Portrait Gallery 9;
Tony Stone (Pauline Cutler) *title page*, 4; Wayland Picture Library 7, 14, 15, 18, 22–3.

Contents

Big wite night

Strange things happen on the fifth of November. As soon as it is dark, bonfires are lit all over Britain.

Everyone wraps up in warm clothes. They go outside to watch fireworks explode like handfuls of jewels thrown into the night sky. Sometimes on top of the bonfire sits a guy. A guy is a dummy made by children.

▲ Many people have parties on Bonfire Night with fireworks and a bonfire.

An important day

People celebrate every fifth of November because of something that happened nearly 400 years ago.

On the 5th of November 1605, a plan to kill the king of England was discovered and stopped. The plan was to blow up the Houses of Parliament while the king was there.

▼ These are the plotters who planned to blow up the Houses of Parliament.

◀ This is what the inside
of the Houses of Parliament
looked like in 1605.

It was called the Gunpowder Plot. Since
then people have celebrated every year
because the plot failed.

Who would want to kill their king? To
answer that question we will have to look
at what was happening 400 years ago.

In those days

Britain 400 years ago was very different from today. Nowadays, people can pray to any god they like.

People living then were told by the king or queen that they must belong to the Church of England.

▼ Today, there are many different religions in Britain. People can pray to any god they like.

◀ King James I.

The king of England at that time was James I.
He was also the leader of the Church of England.

Some people, called Catholics, think that the
Pope should be head of the Church. Catholics
were punished by James I for saying this.

James I was not a popular king. People thought he was ugly and weak. Many Catholics were angry with James I because he would not let them obey the Pope. He treated Catholics harshly.

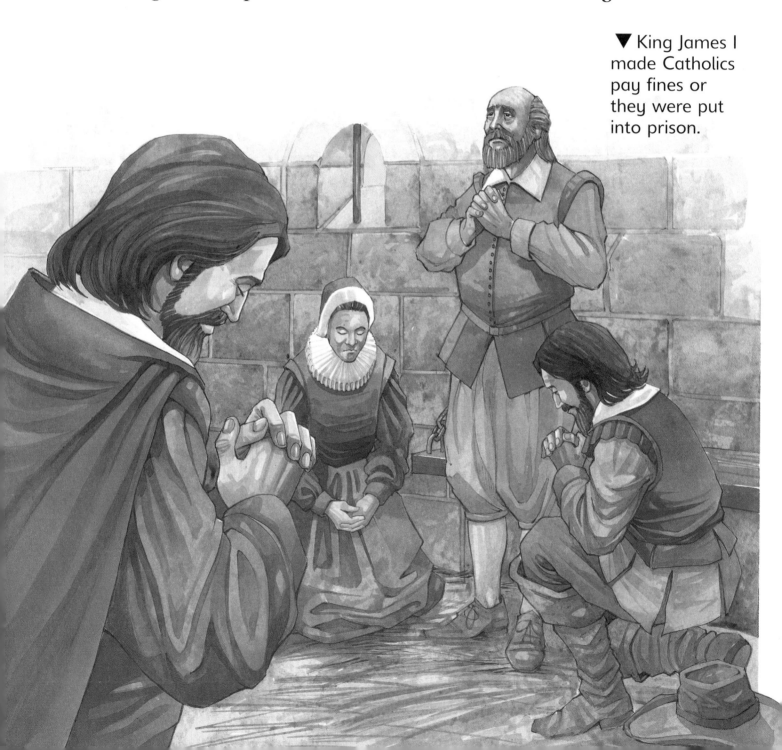

▼ King James I made Catholics pay fines or they were put into prison.

Several Catholic men got together in secret.
They decided that they would try to kill James I.
The Gunpowder Plot had begun.

▼ Catholic priests and bishops were sometimes put to death.

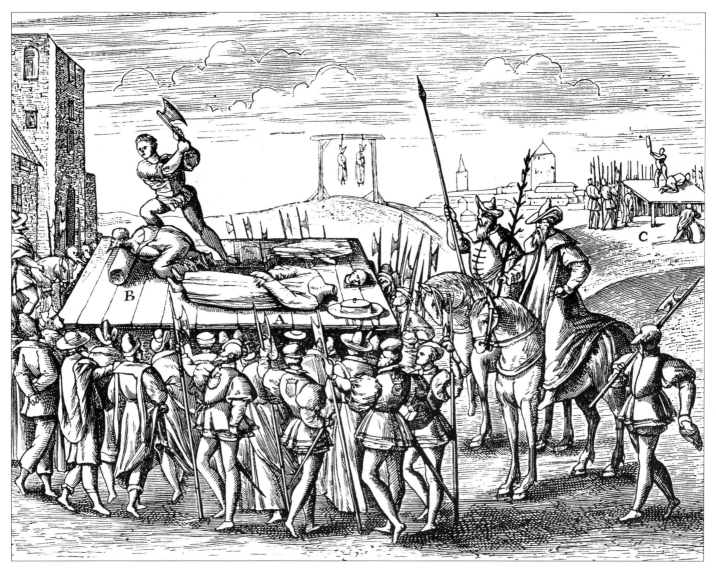

A secret meeting

The man who led the Gunpowder Plot was a Catholic called Robert Catesby. His friends loved him for his kindness. People trusted him. So when he told some friends about his plan, they wanted to join him.

The plotters had a secret meeting. Robert Catesby told them that he planned to blow up the Houses of Parliament using gunpowder. He thought that if the king was killed, then Catholics would no longer be punished.

The plot

▲ Guy Fawkes and Robert Catesby taking the gunpowder by boat to the Houses of Parliament.

Robert Catesby's idea was to put gunpowder underneath the Houses of Parliament and set light to it next time the king went there. One of the plotters, a man called Guy Fawkes, was chosen to set light to the gunpowder.

First the plotters tried to dig a tunnel underneath the Parliament buildings from a house next door. Then they discovered that there was an empty cellar under the Houses of Parliament. They had no need to dig after all.

The plotters put lots of barrels of gunpowder in the cellar. Then they waited for King James I to arrive.

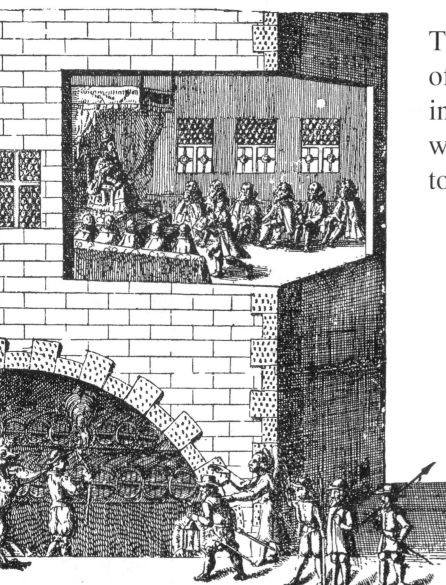

◄ This picture shows King James I in the Houses of Parliament and Guy Fawkes with the gunpowder in the cellar below.

Discovered!

The night before King James was to visit the Houses of Parliament, Guy Fawkes went down into the cellar and prepared to set light to the gunpowder. But the plot had already been found out.

A letter had been sent to a Catholic man, called Lord Monteagle. It warned him not to visit the Houses of Parliament as he would be in danger. The letter was shown to the king.

King James guessed from the letter that someone was going to try to kill him. He ordered his guards to search the Houses of Parliament. In the cellar, the guards found Guy Fawkes. He had his matches ready, and was waiting to light the gunpowder.

▼ Guy Fawkes being arrested by the king's guards.

Guy Fawkes was arrested and taken to the king. He told King James that he was not sorry about what he had done. Guy Fawkes was put in prison in the Tower of London.

The end of the plot

When they heard that the plot had failed, Robert Catesby and the other plotters left London. They leapt on their horses and galloped towards the north of England.

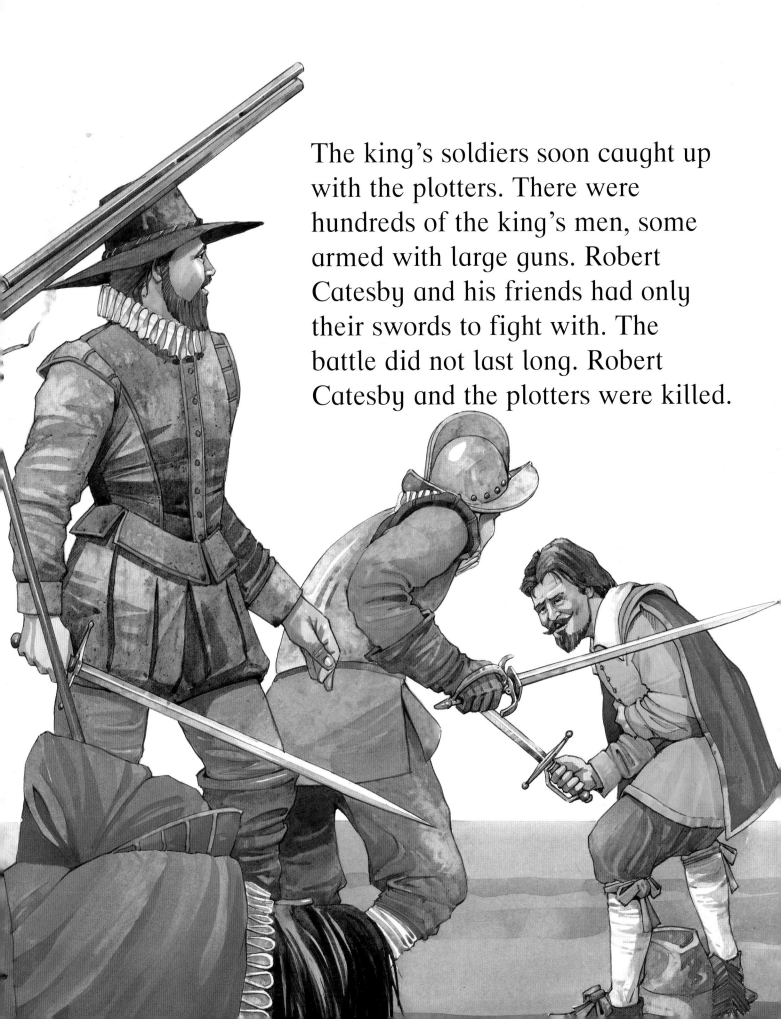

The king's soldiers soon caught up with the plotters. There were hundreds of the king's men, some armed with large guns. Robert Catesby and his friends had only their swords to fight with. The battle did not last long. Robert Catesby and the plotters were killed.

Remember, remember

Guy Fawkes and the rest of the plotters were sent to the Tower of London. Two months later, they were put to death.

The king said that people must not forget the Gunpowder Plot. They must thank God on the fifth of November every year because the plot had failed.

▶ The plotters being dragged through London before being put to death.

Bonfire Night has been a special event ever since.
There is an old rhyme that says

> *Remember, remember, the fifth of November,*
> *Gunpowder, treason and plot.*
> *I see no reason why gunpowder treason*
> *Should ever be forgot.*

Afterwards

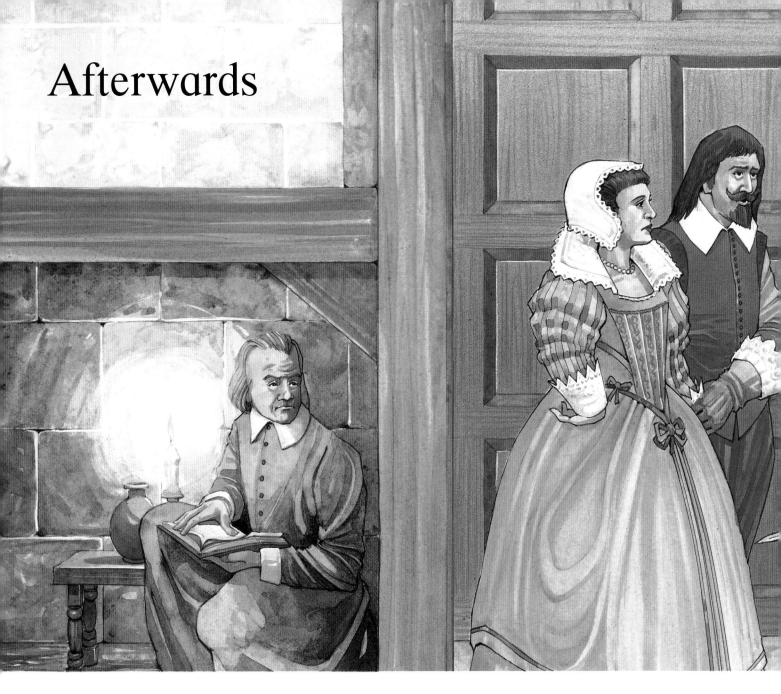

The Gunpowder Plot made King James I even more afraid of Catholic people. He made strict laws about what Catholics could do. They were not allowed to have important jobs like being judges or doctors. They were not allowed to travel away from their homes unless the king said so.

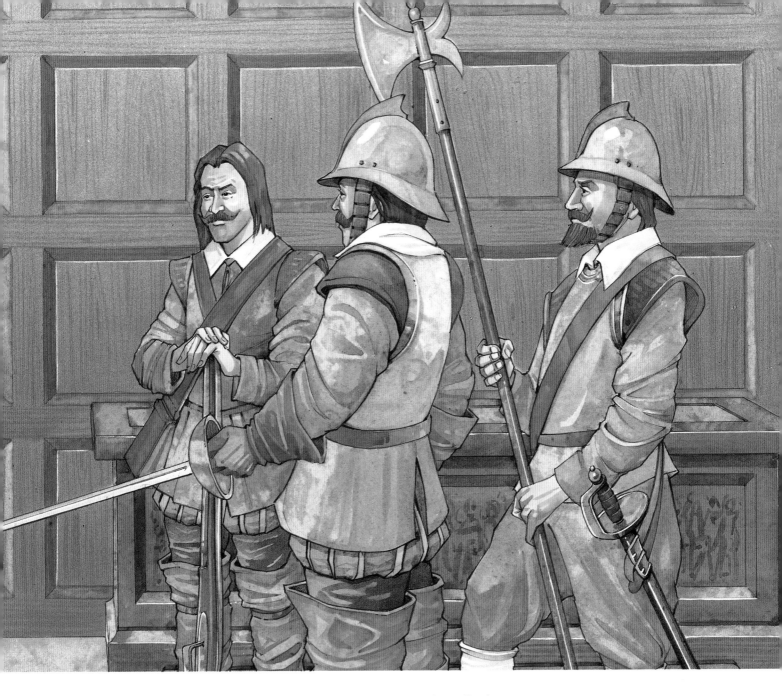

The king or queen is still the head of the Church of England. But today, people are free to be Catholic. There are laws now that try to make sure that people are not treated differently because of their religion.

▲ When King James I ruled Britain, Catholic priests sometimes had to hide in secret passages in friends' houses.

Celebrating Bonfire Night

When the Gunpowder Plot was discovered, people who supported the king made a dummy out of straw to look like Guy Fawkes. Then they burned the 'guy' on top of a huge bonfire.

People have been doing the same thing each year ever since.

In the past, the celebrations used to be much louder and rougher. Gangs of boys used to fight each other for their home-made 'guy'. In a town called Clare, the butchers used to parade the streets making a terrible noise by banging large bones together.

In some towns, there are special celebrations.
The streets of Lewes are filled with people in
fancy dress costumes carrying flaming torches.

▲ People used to roll burning barrels of tar through the streets on Bonfire Night.

▲ Bonfire Night in the town of Bridgewater in Somerset.

For many years, fireworks have been an important part of the celebrations. The powder that explodes in fireworks is the same kind of gunpowder that was used by Guy Fawkes and the plotters.

The bangs, flashes and smoke of the fireworks remind us of what would have happened if Guy Fawkes had managed to light the gunpowder.

Glossary

Catholics   Christians who believe that the leader of the Church is the Pope.

Church of England   The Church that is ruled by the king or queen of England.

Dummy   An image of a person made of straw and cloth.

Fines   Money paid as a punishment.

Gunpowder   A mixture of chemicals that explodes when it is lit.

Houses of Parliament   The buildings in London where Parliament meets. The Houses of Parliament that existed in the time of King James I were different from the buildings that exist on the same spot today.

Pope   The leader of the Catholic Church. He lives in Rome.

Tower of London   A building in London which was used as a prison. It is now a museum.

Treason   To plot against or harm the ruler of your country.

Timeline

1603		James I becomes king.
1604	Feb	Robert Catesby first tells his friends about the plot.
	Dec	Plotters begin to dig a tunnel to the Houses of Parliament.
1605	5 Nov	The Gunpowder Plot is discovered.
1606	Jan	The plotters are executed. James I says the fifth of November is to be a day of thanksgiving.

Further information

Books to read

Guy Fawkes by Clare Chandler (Wayland, 1995)

Stuarts: Craft Topics by Rachel Wright (Watts, 1993)

The Gunpowder Plot by Rhoda Nottridge (Wayland, 1991)

For older readers

Tudors and Stuarts, Family Life by Tessa Hosking (Wayland, 1994)

What Do We Know About the Tudors and Stuarts? by Richard Tames
 (Simon and Schuster, 1994)

Remember!

- Always stand well back from fireworks.
- Never throw fireworks.
- Never put fireworks in your pockets.
- Never play with fireworks.

Index